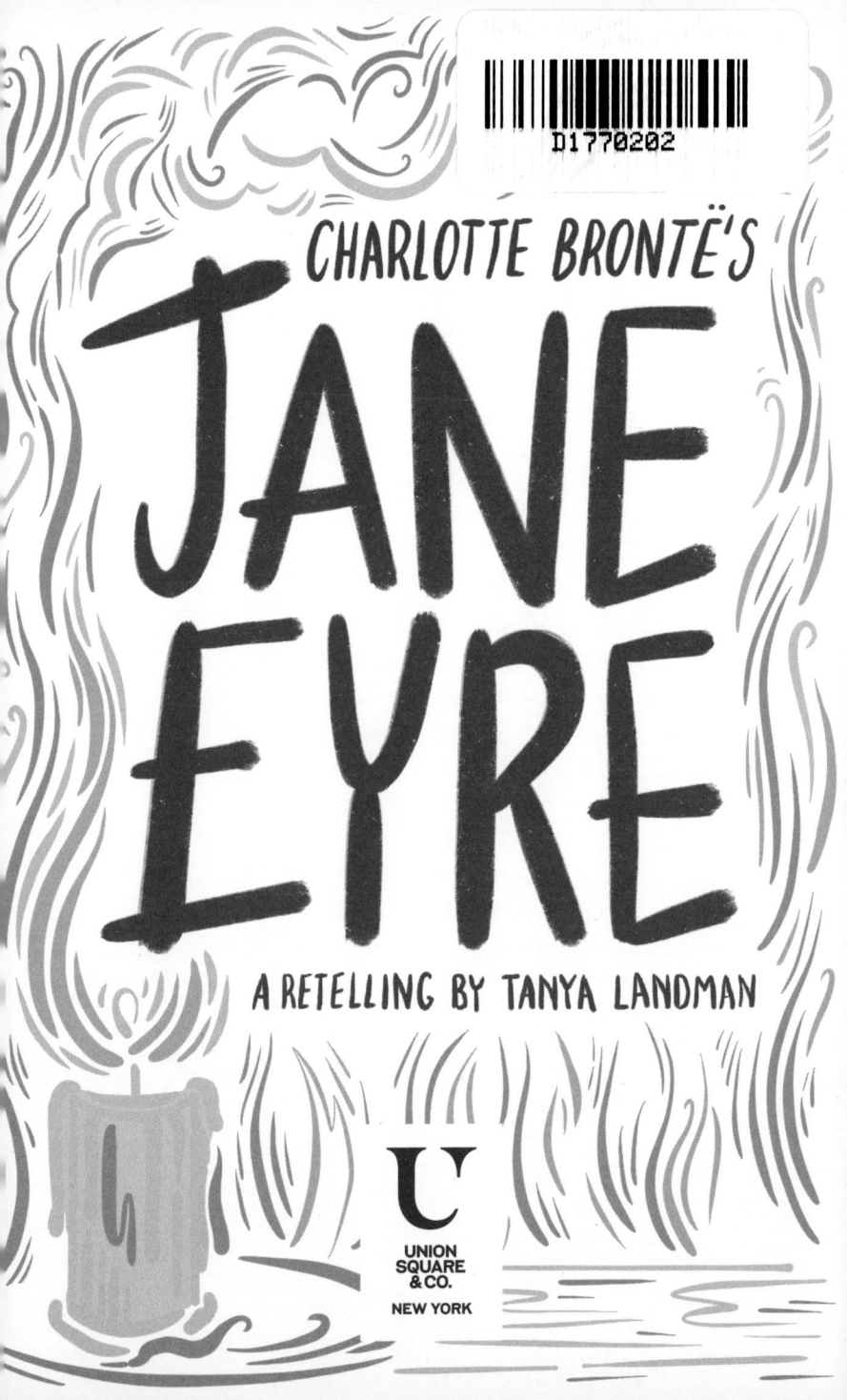

UNION SQUARE & CO.
NEW YORK

UNION SQUARE & CO. and the distinctive Union Square & Co. logo are trademarks of Sterling Publishing Co., Inc.

Union Square & Co., LLC, is a subsidiary of Sterling Publishing Co., Inc.

Text © 2020 Tanya Landman
Cover illustration © 2024 Helen Crawford-White

All rights reserved. No part of this publication may be reproduced, stored in a retrieval system, or transmitted in any form or by any means (including electronic, mechanical, photocopying, recording, or otherwise) without prior written permission from the publisher.

First published in Great Britain in 2020 by Barrington Stoke Ltd. First published in the United States and Canada in 2024 by Union Square & Co., LLC.

ISBN 978-1-4549-5481-1

Library of Congress Control Number: 2023942891

For information about custom editions, special sales, and premium purchases, please contact specialsales@unionsquareandco.com.

Printed in China

2 4 6 8 10 9 7 5 3 1

unionsquareandco.com

Union Square & Co.'s EVERYONE CAN BE A READER books are expertly written, thoughtfully designed with dyslexia-friendly fonts and paper tones, and carefully formatted to meet readers where they are with engaging stories that encourage reading success across a wide range of age and interest levels.

To Isaac and Jack, in the hope that they will finally read Jane Eyre

1.

I was not loved.

I was not wanted.

I did not belong.

I lived with my aunt and cousins, but I was not welcome in their house. My parents had died when I was a baby, and my uncle took me in. He didn't live much longer than they had. I don't remember any of them.

My strange story starts on a wet winter's day. There was no chance of taking a walk, and I was glad of it. I never liked being out with my cousins. They had rosy cheeks, golden hair, and brimmed with the kind of confidence only money can buy. They would stride ahead as we walked, and I'd be stomping along in their shadows. I was small, shabby, and the nursemaid nagged me at every step. The chilly air bit deep into my bones, but what bit even deeper was knowing I was disliked. That clamped its teeth right down into my soul.

The wind blew so hard that wet winter's day the rain fell sideways. No one dared set foot outdoors. My cousins were in the drawing room, clustered around their dear mama. She lay on the sofa, basking in the fire's warmth like a well-fed pig.

I'd been told to go away. I was banished from their company for some sin or other, I don't know what. I asked my aunt what I'd done wrong, but that just made things worse. Children were not meant to question their elders, my aunt said. It was unnatural. Odd. Children were meant to be cheerful and charming. And if they could not be cheerful and charming, they should at least be silent.

Very well, I thought. I walked into the next room and shut the door behind me. I took a book from the shelf, climbed on to the window seat, and pulled the curtains across so I was hidden from sight.

I was all right until my cousin John came looking for me.

John was fourteen years old. He'd been kept home from school these last few weeks because his mother feared he'd been exhausting himself. My aunt adored her son John: he was an angel fallen to earth in her eyes. A genius with the soul of a poet and the heart of a saint. Never has a mother been so mistaken.

John was a selfish bully who cared little for his mother and less for his sisters. I was his one passion. He hated me. John attacked me not two or three times a week, or once or twice a day, but continually. I was four years younger and half his size. Every nerve in my body feared him. Every inch of my flesh shrank whenever he came near.

I heard the door open and I froze. John was not intelligent or observant. He wouldn't have seen me at all if one of his sisters hadn't pointed out my hiding place. He came in, ordered me from the window seat, and demanded, "What were you doing?"

"Reading," I replied.

"Show me the book."

I placed it in his hands.

"You've no right to take our books!" John said. "You're an orphan, a beggar! You've no money. You should be on the streets, not living here at Gateshead, eating our food, wearing clothes my mother has paid for. I'll teach you your place. Go and stand over there, by the door."

I did what I was told. There was no one to turn to for help. The servants could not afford to notice, and my aunt became blind and deaf whenever John raised a hand against me.

He hurled the book. I dodged but too late. The big heavy volume hit me, and I fell, striking my head on the door. The cut bled, and along with the pain I felt a sudden, overwhelming rage. I'd suffered John for nearly ten years. But now I'd had enough!

I'll not say what I called him. It wasn't polite. For a moment John stood gaping. He couldn't believe I'd dared to stand up to him. He was so shocked!

And then he ran at me. His hands grasped my hair, tugging so hard I thought he'd rip my scalp off. Blood ran down my neck, and I truly feared John was going to kill me. I lashed out, grabbing the only part of him I could reach. Digging in my nails I squeezed his soft flesh with all my might.

I didn't know what I'd done. I couldn't even see with my head pulled back. John squealed like a pig, and that brought both my aunt and the maids running.

John and I were dragged apart. I was called a wildcat. A demon. A fiend. And then my aunt told the maids, "Take her to the red room. Lock her in."

2.

The red room.

It was the largest, most splendid, most comfortably furnished of all the rooms in Gateshead House. And yet it was the room where no fire ever burned and no one ever slept. It was the room I would run past if I was alone in the corridor, because of the strange, unearthly air that seemed to seep under the door. My uncle had died in that room, and he'd lain there in his coffin for a week before his burial. That was nine years ago, but the red room still had the feel of a graveyard. The maids had to drag me every inch of the way, but they were two fully grown women and I was a scrawny scrap of a ten-year-old. They got me in there fast and then left me.

A child in a haunted room. My rage turned to terror. The maids had not given me a candle, and the wet winter's day was fast fading to night. I thought every draft was my uncle's ghostly breath, every creak his ghostly bones, the wind howling down the chimney his ghostly wails. My fear grew moment by moment until I could bear it no more.

And then a light flitted across the ceiling. It was probably just someone crossing the lawn outside carrying a storm lantern, but my mind was in no state to be sensible. I was sure that light was my uncle's spirit coming to carry me down to hell.

I screamed, and my screams summoned the maids. But they also summoned my aunt. I wept, I begged for mercy, and I pleaded to be let out, but there was no heart in my aunt to melt. She pushed me back into the room.

I must have had some sort of fit. I remember hearing my aunt's feet going back down along the corridor. But after that? Nothing.

3.

I don't know how long I was locked in the red room. Hours? Days? I've no idea. All I know is that when I woke I was back in my own bed and I was feeling very poorly.

My aunt came to see me. If I'd been apologetic, if I'd begged her forgiveness, things might have worked out between us. All she wanted was for me to be magically transformed into somebody different, someone who was meek and mild and above all pretty. But I'd spent ten years trying to be the child she wanted. The harder I'd tried, the worse I'd failed. I'd had enough of her too.

I told my aunt that John was a spiteful bully and that what she'd done to me was evil. I said she'd burn in hell for being so cruel.

In return, she told me I was a liar, a demon child. She said she would not keep me under her roof a moment longer.

She made arrangements for me to be sent away to school. My heart leaped at the idea. School meant learning to paint and draw and play the piano. It meant learning French and mathematics and reading poetry. School meant freedom. Didn't it?

Maybe to some.

But not to me.

My aunt selected Lowood, a charitable school for orphan girls. Miss Temple was the teacher in charge, and she was kind enough. But Mr. Brocklehurst, the clergyman who held the purse strings, was a tight-fisted ... I'll not say the word that comes to mind. He was tall as a stone pillar and as hard as one too, dressed always in black. He spoke of God and quoted the Bible and threatened us with hellfire and damnation. We girls were poor and therefore undeserving, Mr. Brocklehurst said. We needed to be kept humble. Grateful. We needed to know our place. So we were dressed in clothes that did not keep out the cold and shoes that did not keep out the wet. We slept two to a bed under a single blanket and were fed food of such poor quality in such small portions that staying alive was a struggle. A struggle that a good many of us lost the first year I was there.

School taught me many things, but three stand out in my mind.

The first was that sinners walk among us, disguised as respectable clergymen.

The second was that saints live on earth too—people so good, so pure, with souls that shine so brightly they illuminate everything and everyone around them.

And the third?

Saints die.

4.

I met Helen Burns on my first morning at Lowood. It had been brutally hard. The lessons were bewildering, the rules strict. I did not know the school's routine, and no one took the trouble to explain it to me. By the time we were allowed outside for a breath of fresh air, I was lonely, afraid, and dizzy with hunger.

Helen was sitting alone with a book open on her lap. It was the book that drew me to her, the book that gave me the courage to speak. She was five years older than me and looked like a goddess. And she was kind and gentle, and I was so sorely in need of that. Is it any wonder I was besotted with her?

I could fill this book with praise of Helen Burns and I wouldn't even have begun to describe the beauty of her soul. Let me just say this: I have never met anyone before or since who so truly lived by the words of Jesus Christ. Helen really did love her enemies. She really did bless those who cursed her, and she did good to those who hated and despised her. I admired Helen. But she totally baffled me.

5.

That first winter at Lowood was as harsh as anything I've ever known. I raged against Mr. Brocklehurst the whole time. The fury burning inside my chest carried me through those dreadful months. Helen survived them without a murmur of complaint because she had Christ-like powers of endurance.

Even the longest, hardest winter has to end eventually.

At last, the warm air of spring breathed life into the woods around the school. Pinpricks of emerald green appeared on the beech trees. The ground was carpeted with bluebells and primroses.

That same warm air of spring breathed typhus fever into the crowded classrooms and turned our school into a hospital. We were half starved and weakened by months of extreme cold. The disease raged through Lowood's inmates like a fire. More than half the girls were taken ill.

But I was not one of them. The typhus meant there were no lessons, so I was allowed to roam freely outside from dawn till dusk. Mr. Brocklehurst dared not come near Lowood for fear of catching our disease, so there was no talk of hell or damnation. I was oddly contented. Yet Helen was not beside me. She was ill, but not with the fever. I'd been told she had consumption and, being a child who knew nothing about medical matters, I thought she'd recover soon.

One day I'd helped myself to bread and cheese from the kitchen and gone out, roaming farther even than normal. The day was so bright and clear I suddenly broke down in tears. I was thinking about how sad it must be to be lying ill, to be dying, when life was so lovely and the world so beautiful.

When I got back to Lowood, it was already dark and I saw the doctor riding away. The maid was still at the door, and I asked, "How is Helen Burns?"

"Poorly," the maid replied. "But she'll not be here much longer."

They were sending Helen back to her family, I thought. I knew she had an aunt and uncle somewhere. I wanted to say goodbye, but they wouldn't let me speak to her, no matter how I pleaded. So in the middle of that night—when everyone slept—I crept along the dark corridors.

When I found her, she was lying in bed looking as calm and serene as ever.

"Jane!" Helen said gently. "Your feet are bare. Come here. Cover yourself with my quilt."

I nestled in beside her.

"I'm going home," Helen whispered.

"I heard," I said. "Where does your family live? York?"

"No! Not to them." Helen's breath was warm in my hair. "I'm going home to God."

I let out a strangled gasp. I struggled to believe her. How could anyone be close to death and not rage against it?

But this was not anyone: it was Helen Burns. Heaven wasn't a matter of hope or faith with her. It was a matter of solid, rational fact. It was as if Helen could see the gates of heaven right there, open wide, ready to receive her. And perhaps she could. She had a soft glow to her, a blissful happiness I could not understand.

I think Helen thought I envied her, because as she stroked my hair she said, "You will come to heaven too in time, dear Jane. Never doubt it."

But I did. Where was it? Did it exist?

I said nothing.

Helen was so tired. She pulled me close and we both drifted off to sleep.

When Miss Temple came in at dawn, she found the two of us, arms around each other. I was still fast asleep.

Helen was dead.

6.

The typhus fever that swept through Lowood carried away so many of its inmates that it couldn't be ignored. So many poor orphans were buried in the churchyard that even the high and mighty noticed. They asked questions. They demanded answers. How had this come about? Who was to blame?

Mr. Brocklehurst was a rich and powerful man. (The "blessed are the poor" line in the Bible had somehow escaped his attention.) He could not be removed from his position at Lowood, but he could be overseen. A committee was set up to manage the school, and life there became bearable.

I did well. At Gateshead, I'd tried so hard to please my aunt, but every effort had just made things worse. At Lowood the opposite was true. The harder I worked and the more effort I made, the more I was rewarded and respected.

I stayed there for eight years—six as a pupil and two as a teacher. I was not unhappy. Lowood was the closest thing I had to a home.

But then Miss Temple got married. She'd been my most excellent teacher, my patient guide, and my dear friend. After the wedding ceremony, when the happy couple stepped into a carriage and disappeared over the hill, my contentment went with her.

I retired to my room and started pacing the floorboards. For eight years I'd tried to follow in the footsteps of my saintly friend, Helen. It all fell away in the space of one afternoon. I was no Helen Burns. I saw this world, not the next. I did not have one foot in heaven—both of mine were rooted to the earth.

I wanted excitement. I was restless. A hunger awoke in me—it itched under my skin. The world was wide and wonderful and I had seen so little of it. I wanted freedom. I was desperate to stretch my wings, to fly.

How foolish an ambition was that? Did I not know my place? I wasn't a lady of fortune who could travel as I wished. I was a nothing, a nobody. I must earn my keep, pay my way. I needed to be reasonable.

Not freedom then, I told myself. Nothing so large. But perhaps a different kind of imprisonment? Another place, a new position. Yes ... that would do.

And so I set the wheels of change in motion.

I placed an advertisement in the newspaper:

A young lady accustomed to teaching is seeking a situation with a family where the children are under fourteen. She is qualified to teach the usual branches of a good English education, together with French, Drawing, and Music.

A week later, I received a reply. A Mrs. Fairfax of Thornfield Hall wanted a governess for one pupil—a girl aged seven.

Letters were written. References were sent. And not two months after Miss Temple had married I found myself leaving Lowood for the first and last time.

7.

I left Lowood before dawn. I arrived at Thornfield Hall long after the sun had set, near exhausted from a day of traveling. I had the impression of a large house but could see little of it. A maid named Mary showed me to a snug parlor where a fire burned bright in the grate. An elderly lady sat knitting beside it, a cat curled at her feet.

"Mrs. Fairfax?" I asked.

"Yes!" she said, and stood, insisting I sit in her chair so I could warm myself. She sent Mary running to the kitchen for food, for she was sure I must be hungry. I was overcome with relief. I'd launched myself into the unknown and it looked like I'd found a safe landing.

That night I climbed into a warmed bed in a room that I had all to myself. Being alone was the most incredible luxury. For six years at Lowood I'd been in a dormitory with a dozen other girls. For the next two I'd shared a bedroom with a fellow teacher whose grunting and snoring had kept me awake.

I stretched my limbs, I shut my eyes, and I fell into a sleep so deep it was close to death.

8.

I'd assumed Thornfield Hall belonged to Mrs. Fairfax and that my pupil was her grandchild, but I was wrong on both counts. She was the housekeeper. The owner was a Mr. Rochester who was rarely at home, Mrs. Fairfax told me the next day. My pupil was his ward, a little French girl called Adèle Varens.

I met Adèle at breakfast. She was a pretty thing—small with dainty features and a vast mane of curling dark hair that fell down to her waist. I could speak French fluently, for the teacher at Lowood had been a native of the country and I'd studied long and hard to perfect my accent. When Adèle discovered this, the words flowed from her in a stream that I feared might never end.

I learned that her mother, Cécile Varens, had been a dancer who'd died and gone to live with the Holy Virgin. Mr. Rochester had been Cécile's very,

very dear friend and had asked Adèle if she wanted to come and live with him in England. She'd said yes because he'd always been kind and brought her pretty dresses and toys, and he'd carried her over the sea in a ship that smoked. She'd been sick and so had Mr. Rochester, and now he hadn't kept his word because he was never here!

I'd been buried at Lowood for eight years, but I was not entirely ignorant of the ways of the world. I didn't think it was possible that a rich man would care for the daughter of a dancer unless he was the father of her child. But it was not my place to ask questions.

After we'd eaten, Adèle and I retired to the library to begin her lessons. She was sweet-tempered and very willing to please but unused to the efforts of learning. By noon, Adèle was exhausted, and I thought it best to let her go back to the nursery with her maid.

I was about to begin a painting, but then Mrs. Fairfax offered to show me the house and I accepted.

We went from one large, splendid room stuffed with paintings, tapestries, and fine furniture to another. The master might rarely be at home, but Mrs. Fairfax kept everything spotless and ready for his arrival. Mr. Rochester never, ever gave her advance warning that he was coming, she said. He just turned up.

Once we'd finished the grand tour, she wanted to show me the view from the roof. She led me up a narrow staircase to the third floor, a part of the house she said was unoccupied. From there we climbed up a ladder and through a trapdoor.

We emerged on a level with the rooks' nests. The view was indeed magnificent. I saw a church tower not half a mile away. A lane leading to the village. The grounds spread out below, where nature was cut and clipped and caged. And beyond, the wild, untamed moor.

I came back down the ladder, leaving Mrs. Fairfax to bolt the trapdoor. I'd reached the narrow staircase when a strange sound struck my ears.

Laughter. Laughter without a trace of joy. Laughter without amusement.

It came again. Low. Chilling. Empty.

"Mrs. Fairfax!" I said. "Did you hear that?"

She wasn't concerned. "It's Grace Poole," she said. "One of the maids. She sews, sometimes, in one of these rooms."

The laugh came again.

"Grace!" Mrs. Fairfax called.

I did not expect anyone to answer. It was such a strange and supernatural sound that I'd almost convinced myself it was a ghost. But then a door opened and a woman came out. Behind her I saw an almost empty room with only a single chair and a huge tapestry covering one wall. Then she slammed the door shut and stood squarely in front of it, arms folded. This was Grace Poole. She was thirty, perhaps forty years old, small and squat with a red nose set in a face as plain as my own.

"You're making too much noise," Mrs. Fairfax told her.

"Very sorry, madam." Grace Poole's eyes darted sideways at me, then back to Mrs. Fairfax. I felt something had been said in the look that passed between them. Grace bobbed a curtsy, but she didn't go back into the room until after Mrs. Fairfax and I had left the corridor.

While we walked down to the ground floor, Mrs. Fairfax asked me how Adèle had fared with her lessons that morning. And soon Adèle herself appeared, running across the hall toward us. She declared it was time to eat and she was half dead from hunger and where had we been?

Nothing more was said of Grace Poole.

9.

I had found a truly comfortable situation. Adèle was no genius, but she was perfectly easy to teach. Mrs. Fairfax was no great conversationalist, but she was perfectly pleasant company. I should have been content, but I wasn't.

Why?

I was young. I wanted excitement. I needed to live, not simply exist.

I couldn't sit still by the fire while Mrs. Fairfax chattered about nothing night after night. Instead, after Adèle was tucked up in bed, I'd go to the third-floor corridor. There I paced back and forth, back and forth. I was praying, wishing, *dying* for something to happen. Anything.

Up there I sometimes heard Grace Poole's laugh—that same empty, joyless sound that chilled my blood every single time. Sometimes Grace murmured to herself, but I could never catch the words. Once in a while I passed her on the stairs, but she never spoke to me.

One evening she was carrying a pot of ale from the kitchen. A drinker then, I thought. The beer explained her ruddy face. But it did not entirely explain the strangeness of the noises Grace made in that room. It did not explain why no one else ever commented on them. And I was surprised that a housekeeper as careful as Mrs. Fairfax would allow a drunk to be in Mr. Rochester's employment.

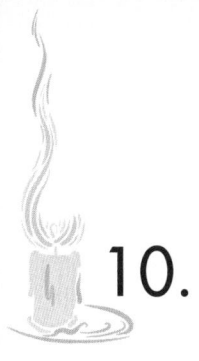

10.

Three months passed very, very slowly. A fourth month began. We were more than halfway through it when Adèle was taken ill.

She had a cold, nothing more, but she made the most of it. After our midday meal, she declared she could not possibly have any more lessons! She threw herself on the floor and wailed that she was ill. She said she was dying like her poor dear mother! Oh! She could hear the Holy Virgin calling to her!

I had no pity, but Mrs. Fairfax was kinder and more trusting than me. Adèle was wrapped in a blanket and placed on a sofa in front of the fire. And I found myself with an unexpected afternoon of freedom.

Mrs. Fairfax needed a letter mailed, so I offered to walk the two miles to the village.

It was cold and crisp outside, the ground hard underfoot and every puddle turned to ice. Frost hung from spiderwebs, turning them to strings of diamonds in the hedges. My breath came in billowing clouds as if I were a mighty dragon in a fairy tale.

I walked slowly, enjoying my solitude.

The lane ran uphill to the village, and after a mile I sat down to rest on some steps. The church bell chimed. Four o'clock. It would not be long until dark, but a full moon was rising behind the trees. Its light would guide me once the sun had gone. It was the kind of enchanted twilight in which goblins danced and fairies cast their spells. Still. Perfect.

And then the crows were calling to each other as if something had alarmed them.

I heard a clatter of hooves coming fast downhill. A demon come to snatch my soul?

No. A horse with a human rider came round the corner, an enormous dog running ahead. I sat still while the three of them passed.

I was about to go on my way when I heard iron slide over ice. Horse's hooves, legs giving way. Falling. Falling hard. The rider crushed, the horse groaning, the dog barking, barking, barking. The noise echoed across the valley, bouncing from hill to hill.

The horse got to its feet, but the rider didn't. The dog ran toward me, tail wagging, yelping, as if asking for help.

I followed it down the lane.

"Are you hurt?" I asked the rider. "Can I help?"

"No," he said. "Stand back. Go away."

Go away? I'd had enough of being told to go away at my aunt's. I was going nowhere.

I stood watching. Very slowly, the rider struggled upright. "It's nothing," he said. "Not broken, just a sprain." But when he tried to put weight on his foot he couldn't.

I might have found it uncomfortable being alone with a strange man—if he'd been young and handsome, or if he'd been friendly or grateful for my concern. But the rider was none of those things. And he'd annoyed me. I offered to fetch help, but he wouldn't let me. He waved me away again, but I refused to go.

"I can't leave until you're back on your horse, nice and safe," I said.

"Safe?" The rider laughed. "What about you? A young woman out alone? Why aren't you at home? Or do you not have one to go to?"

"I have a home," I said. "I live at Thornfield Hall."

"Whose house is that?"

"Mr. Rochester's."

"And who are you?"

"The governess."

The rider grunted and told me to bring his horse to him. But the horrible creature danced out of reach and threw its head up so I could not catch the reins.

"Come back," the rider called. "I must use you as a walking stick." I did as he asked, and he laid his great paw of a hand on my shoulder, digging his fingers right in. We limped toward his animal. And for its master the damned horse stood quietly and lowered its head. I cursed under my breath as the rider managed to get back in the saddle, inch by painful inch.

"Pilot!" he said to the dog. "Let's be on our way." With barely a word of thanks to me, he was gone.

I walked slowly on to the village, mailed the letter, and then walked even more slowly back. I was dreading going into the house and feeling that dreary, smothering boredom wrap itself around me.

But the moment I crossed the threshold, I felt something had changed.

I could hear Adèle chattering feverishly, and another voice. It was low, deep. I couldn't make out any words. Was it a doctor's?

I went looking for Mrs. Fairfax, but she wasn't in the parlor.

Beside her empty chair an enormous dog was sitting by the fire.

"Pilot?" I said.

He wagged his tail and came to lick my hand as if I were a dear and trusted friend.

A prickle of excitement ran down my back as I stroked the dog's ears. It seemed my prayers had been answered at last. Something was going to happen. Good or bad? I didn't know.

I didn't much care.

11.

The master of Thornfield Hall was home. Mr. Rochester was with the doctor when I returned from the village, and then he had an early night. Mary informed me he'd fallen from his horse and sprained an ankle. Clearly he'd not said a word about meeting me in the lane. I was so insignificant that he'd forgotten my existence the moment he was back in the saddle.

I didn't see Mr. Rochester that night, nor the next morning. But the house felt so very different. Those long, echoing corridors and vast empty rooms had felt as cold and silent as a crypt these last months. Now there were knocks at the door, the bell clanged, people came calling. The heart of the house had begun to beat, and life was flowing through its veins. I loved it.

That morning Adèle and I had to move our little school from the library to a room upstairs, but she was impossible to teach that day. Her mind could focus on nothing but the presents her dear, darling Mr. Rochester might bring her.

The day passed. Adèle and I ate our evening meal in the parlor as usual. But then Mrs. Fairfax informed me that the three of us were to take tea with the master in the drawing room at six o'clock.

"You'd better change your dress," Mrs. Fairfax told me.

So this was how it was going to be, was it? Dressing for the evening? Summoned to an audience with the master of Thornfield Hall? Well, I knew my place, didn't I? Lowood had taught me to be grateful for whatever crumbs were thrown in my direction. I did what I was told.

I replaced my black dress with another that was just as plain and simple. I had only three dresses, and the third was one I'd made for Miss Temple's wedding. I'd not worn it since. It was a light gray that sucked up stains and was suitable only for the grandest of occasions. My single piece of jewelry was a brooch Miss Temple had given me. I pinned it on my dress and down I went.

Adèle was already in the drawing room, playing in front of the fire with Pilot.

The rider I'd helped back onto his horse—master of the house and my employer, Mr. Rochester—sat in a chair close by.

The dog greeted me. The man did not. He knew I'd come in, but despite summoning me here himself Mr. Rochester chose to ignore me.

"Miss Eyre is here, sir," Mrs. Fairfax said gently.

"Sit," was his only reply. He didn't even look up.

Rude? Abrupt? Yes. But when were the gentry anything else to their underlings? Courtesy and kindness from him would have made me more uncomfortable—I wouldn't have known how to respond.

I sat down. Mr. Rochester said nothing. Nor did I. Mrs. Fairfax started prattling on about this and that, clearly desperate to fill the yawning silence. She spoke about the weather, mainly. The way the damp autumn had caused mold to grow in the corners of the pantry. How the icy chill had turned a dozen cabbages in the kitchen garden black.

Perhaps to silence her, Mr. Rochester demanded tea. Mrs. Fairfax poured a cup but told me to give it to him.

As he took it my fingertips brushed against his.

Just one touch. So slight. And yet his whole body stiffened.

Mr. Rochester's eyes flicked up and met mine across the steaming teacup. They were dark, piercing, burning with a raging fury that was so familiar it was like looking in a mirror. And then there was something else too. Something I didn't understand. A bright flash at the back of his brain that lit his eyes like a falling firework.

Could that be hope?

Adèle's head had been full of nothing but presents all day. I'd forbidden her to ask Mr. Rochester about anything he might bring her. So the sly little minx suddenly said, "Have you brought a gift for Miss Eyre?"

He glanced at Adèle, wincing as if seized by a painful memory. Suddenly, clear as clear, I could picture Mr. Rochester with Adèle's mother. Dropping furs and silks and jewels into Cécile Varens's lap. Buying himself into her bed.

"You like presents, do you, Miss Eyre?" Mr. Rochester said coldly.

"I've not had much experience of them," I replied. "But people generally find presents nice, don't they?"

"I'm not asking about people, I'm asking about you."

Mr. Rochester carried on staring at me, waiting for me to say more.

"Is a present a pleasant thing?" I said. "I suppose it depends on why it's given. And what the giver expects in return."

"Adèle feels entitled to a great many gifts," Mr. Rochester said. "Do you?"

"Why would I? I'm a stranger to you, sir. I've done nothing that would entitle me to anything."

"False modesty!" he replied. "I've been talking to Adèle and you've worked hard with her. She's much improved."

"That's all the gift I need then," I said. "All any teacher wants is praise for a pupil's progress."

Mr. Rochester grunted and fell into a moody silence.

After the tea tray was taken away, he began to grill me in detail about my past life.

When I told Mr. Rochester I'd been at Lowood, he pounced like a cat on a mouse. "Aha!" he said. "Confined in an institution for eight years ... No wonder you look as if you're from another world. When I saw you last night, I thought of elves and sprites. You looked as if you'd stepped out of a fairy tale. Were you waiting for your people on those steps?"

"My people?" I asked.

"The little ones—the elves and sprites. It was a moonlit evening. Did I break your fairy ring? Is that why you spread that damned ice on the lane?"

I shook my head. "The little people left England long ago," I replied. "You won't find a trace of them, not even at full moon."

Mrs. Fairfax stopped her knitting, clearly confused about the strange turn our conversation had taken.

Mr. Rochester carried on with his questions, ordering me to the piano, then silencing me with a wave of his hand, telling me I played it like a schoolgirl. He demanded I fetch my portfolio so he could see how well I painted. He discarded most of my efforts, throwing them to the floor with a sneer. But three paintings I'd done during those long, lonely holidays at Lowood caught his attention. They were strange scenes: images that had dropped into my head from nowhere. One was of a shipwreck with a bird perched on the mast, a gold bracelet clutched in its beak. The arm the bracelet had been plucked from was disappearing beneath the waves. The second painting was of a woman walking in twilight, her forehead crowned with a star. The third showed an iceberg, a colossal head resting against it that was bloodless and as white as bone.

Mr. Rochester looked at the paintings closely for a long time. And then he asked, "Were you happy when you painted these?"

"I was absorbed and, yes, happy, I suppose."

"And were you satisfied with your work?"

"No!" I said. "The gulf between the picture in my head and what I could set down on the paper tormented me!"

"They are strange. Elfish," Mr. Rochester said softly. He seemed to be talking more to himself than me. "What kind of mind created such images? Those eyes—how did you make them look so clear? And who taught you to paint wind?"

Then he stared at me so hard! His fingers twitched, as if he wanted to break open my head and examine the contents of my brain. And all of a sudden he snapped, "Put them away."

I'd just finished tying the portfolio's strings when Mr. Rochester said, "It's past nine o'clock. Why have you let Adèle stay up so long? Take her to bed."

Our audience was over. We were dismissed.

I retired to bed that night feeling like he'd stripped me bare. My soul was lying naked and exposed at Mr. Rochester's feet. But I knew nothing whatsoever about him.

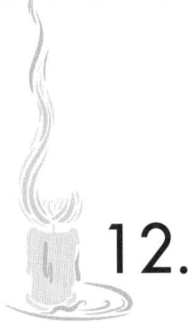

12.

I hardly saw Mr. Rochester for the next few days. We met in the corridor occasionally. Sometimes he'd look straight past me as if I weren't there. Other times he'd bow as if I were his guest, not his governess. I didn't find his shifting moods troubling. They were like a change in the weather or the turning of the river's tide: natural forces that were beyond my control.

About a week after he'd arrived, we were summoned downstairs again. The present that Adèle had waited for so impatiently had finally been delivered. A large box was standing on the table, wrapped in paper and tied with a ribbon.

Adèle gave a shriek of delight.

"Take it away, you true daughter of Paris," Mr. Rochester said to her. "Butcher it on the sofa over there. But I want no running commentary on what you find in its entrails."

He ordered Mrs. Fairfax to keep Adèle company. I, meanwhile, was commanded to a chair uncomfortably near his own.

Mr. Rochester wouldn't let me move my chair back, but then he just sat looking into the fire, ignoring me. I studied his face, refusing to break the silence. He was an ugly brute of a man with a great jutting forehead, a hooked nose, and a square jaw. It looked like a bold, determined face, yet he seemed to burn with some mysterious torment.

Suddenly he turned and caught me staring.

"Do you think me handsome?" Mr. Rochester asked.

"No, sir!" I said, startled into honesty.

"You're very blunt for a governess," he said.

"I beg your pardon. I should have said beauty is in the eye of the beholder."

"You should have said no such thing!" exclaimed Mr. Rochester. "You look so meek, so mild—like you couldn't hurt a fly. And yet you stick your little penknife in right under my ribs." His eyes were brighter than usual. Perhaps he'd drunk too much wine at dinner? He was certainly in a strange, provoking mood. He suddenly demanded to know what faults I found in him: what was wrong with his eyes, his chin, his nose, his forehead? Were his arms and legs long enough? His chest shapely? Or was it his mind I found ugly? Did I think him a fool?

"Far from it," I replied. "But can I ask, sir—are you a kind man?"

"She sticks her penknife in again!" Mr. Rochester laughed, but there was as much bitterness in it as amusement. "Life has beaten the kindness out of me," he went on. "But maybe somewhere, deep inside, a nugget remains. Is there any hope for me?"

"Hope of what?" I asked.

He didn't answer. He threw himself back in the chair. "I wanted company tonight. Speak."

"What about?"

"Anything."

If he wanted me to talk just for the sake of it, he'd chosen the wrong woman. I stayed silent.

Mr. Rochester's voice softened. "Please," he begged. "Talk to me. Distract my thoughts. They're swirling around my head like poison."

"I don't know what to talk about," I said. "You introduce a subject. Ask me questions. I'll answer them."

The strangest conversation followed. Mr. Rochester talked in riddles that made no sense. It was like being in a dance and not knowing the steps. I could see he was deeply troubled and that some secret sorrow haunted him. But he couldn't or wouldn't tell me what it was and so how could I help? He talked of error and regret, of guilt and reform. He asked me if he might be saved. I hardly knew how to answer him. I fell back on the kinds of things that Helen had said to me when I raved with fury about my aunt or Mr. Brocklehurst. Helen had always talked of God's goodness, so I did the same, but I was out of my depth and sinking fast.

It was a relief when the clock struck nine. I got to my feet, meaning to take Adèle up to bed, but she was not on the sofa. It was covered in tissue paper and a great pile of pretty things. It seemed that she'd unearthed a dress at the bottom of the box and had slipped away to put it on.

I could hear Adèle coming across the hall and suddenly she burst into the room wearing a pink dress and satin slippers. A wreath of roses circled her head.

"The very image of Cécile!" Mr. Rochester said quietly. There was scorn, not affection, in his voice.

Adèle danced across the room, blissfully unaware of it. She simpered, twirled, dropped onto one knee at his feet in an elaborate curtsy. Mr.

Rochester seemed to be in real physical pain when he looked at her.

Was Adèle's mother the cause of his torment, I wondered. Was Adèle—the poor child—a constant reminder of Cécile?

And then a third thought tiptoed across my mind. How did she die? What killed her?

13.

Weeks turned into months and the master of Thornfield Hall stayed home, much to Mrs. Fairfax's surprise.

A governess occupies a strange, lonely position in a great house. She is not a maid or a master but somewhere in between. She can be friends with neither but must keep herself to herself. I had to remind myself of that constantly—because the more I was summoned to talk to Mr. Rochester, the more comfortable I felt in his company. I was in great danger of forgetting my place.

He spoke to me as if I were his equal, not his paid servant. He had a dry wit and would tease me with nonsense about elves and sprites. He'd make me laugh with his biting observations. But more often he'd make me think. We'd discuss science and philosophy and literature. Before Mr. Rochester had returned to Thornfield Hall, any conversation I'd had was confined to trivialities. Now I felt my mind breathe and expand: it basked in the warmth of his attention. Is it any wonder I craved his company? And did I still think him ugly? No. Mr. Rochester's face became the one I most liked to see. His presence in a room cheered me more than the brightest of fires.

Winter gave way to spring, and one morning he joined Adèle and me in the gardens. Adèle ran ahead playing with a shuttlecock while Mr. Rochester confided in me about her mother. Their story was nothing remarkable—just a rich young Englishman besotted with a beautiful French dancer. Cécile had been Mr. Rochester's mistress, she'd betrayed him, and then she'd abandoned their child. Mr. Rochester had thought it would be easier for Adèle to believe her mother was dead than know that she'd been cast away like a piece of garbage. He spoke of the affair with humor, not anger. Whatever tormented him, I thought, it was not Cécile Varens.

When Mr. Rochester had finished his tale, he looked back at the house. For a moment, pain, shame, revulsion, and fear took hold of his features, twisting his face into something that looked barely human.

14.

When I retired to bed that night, Mr. Rochester's face was still imprinted on my eyelids. I blew out my candle, but I couldn't sleep. The clock struck two. And then I heard a faint noise, like fingers sliding across the door of my chamber.

No ... not fingers ... Don't be silly, I told myself. It's Pilot, that's all. He's broken his kennel chain and is sneaking up to his master's room again.

But then there was a laugh—low, demonic, closer than I'd ever heard it—as if a mouth was at my keyhole.

I heard the handle turn. Leaping from my bed, I bolted the door.

"Who's there?" I demanded.

No answer, but footsteps slowly padded toward the third-floor staircase.

Grace Poole, I thought. It must be. Terror had seized me by the throat. I tried to talk myself out of it, but I failed. I couldn't bear to be alone in the dark. I decided to go to Mrs. Fairfax.

When I opened my door, there was a candle standing on the floor outside. In its flickering light, I saw the door of Mr. Rochester's room was ajar. A whisper of smoke came curling out.

I was in there in a heartbeat. Flames were licking over the bed; the drapes were ablaze. I tried shaking Mr. Rochester, but he was overcome by smoke. The basin and jug in his room were both large and both mercifully full of water. I heaved first one and then the other over and soaked the bed and its occupant. It was not enough. I ran back to my own room, grabbed my water jug, and threw the contents over my master.

At last Mr. Rochester stirred. But he wasn't in the best of moods to find himself lying in the pitch dark in a pool of water. A stream of curses spilled from his mouth.

"What's happening?" he asked. "Is there a flood?"

"No," I said.

"Jane Eyre?" he said. "Have you tried to drown me, witch?"

"Somebody's tried something, but not me." I fetched the candle from the corridor. He took it from my hand and examined the burnt drapes, the charred mattress. I'd never seen Mr. Rochester look so grim.

He wouldn't let me wake Mrs. Fairfax or call any of the maids. Instead, he told me to wrap myself in his cloak, to sit in his chair, and to wait for his return. And then he took the candle and headed down the corridor, leaving me alone in the cold and the dark.

In the red room, all my terrors had been imagined. This was real. Something evil had stalked the corridors of Thornfield Hall. And it might come back.

It seemed a very long time indeed before Mr. Rochester returned.

He was looking very pale, and the candle shook in his hand. He set it down.

"Tell me," Mr. Rochester said. "When you opened your door ... did you see anything?"

"Only the candle," I replied. "But before that I heard a laugh."

He sat down on the sodden bed.

"I've heard it before," I said. "There's a woman who sews here. Grace Poole—she makes that horrible noise."

Mr. Rochester's frown became a little less deep, but he was still pale and shaken. "That's right," he said, nodding. "Grace Poole. I'll deal with her in the morning. But you're to say nothing of this, do you hear?" He stared at me and then laughed. "What am I saying? Look at that face! I know you're no gossip. I can trust you to keep quiet. Go to bed, Jane. Sleep if you can."

I was dismissed. I stood up.

Mr. Rochester looked surprised. "You're going?" he asked.

"You told me to," I said. But he seemed to have forgotten that.

"You can't go! Not without saying a proper good night. You saved my life!" He reached out a hand. I gave him mine, and he took it in both his own. He held it so tight I feared he might break my fingers. "I owe you such a debt," he said.

A rising tide of feeling threatened to engulf me. "There is no debt," I replied. "I'm owed nothing."

Mr. Rochester's voice was shaking. "I knew you'd save me in some way, at some time. I knew it when I saw you sitting on those steps. God placed you there; he sent you to rescue me. I knew that very night that the sight of you did not delight my heart for nothing."

Strange energy was in his voice, a strange fire in his eyes. I could not bear to hold his gaze; it was overwhelming. I would lose myself in him. And I must not. He was the master, I was his hired hand. His paid servant. I was nothing.

Know your place, my aunt's voice rang inside my head.

Know your place, Mr. Brocklehurst's words echoed in my chest.

Know your place, eight years of Lowood's teaching poured through my veins.

I averted my eyes, I tried to go, but still Mr. Rochester would not release my hand. "I'm cold," I said.

"Cold?" he replied. "Yes ... and soaking wet. Go then. Leave me." But still he would not let go.

"I think Mrs. Fairfax is stirring, sir," I said. Her name was enough to remind him of the order of things. At last he dropped my hand, and I returned to my room.

There was no chance of sleep. My emotions were too stirred up for me to rest. I was out of bed and dressed as soon as day dawned.

15.

I expected Mr. Rochester to come to the schoolroom that morning. He did not.

I expected him to summon me to the library. No command came.

I was going down for lunch when I passed his bedroom. Mary and another maid had been cleaning in there all morning, and I wanted to know what they'd been told about the fire. I put my head around the door and saw a third person in the room.

Grace Poole, calmly sewing rings onto new curtains.

Why was she still in the house? And why were the other maids laughing and chatting with her so easily? She was evil, and no one but me seemed to know it.

"Good morning, miss," Grace said. Her face gave nothing away.

"What happened here?" I asked Mary.

Grace answered. "The master was reading in bed last night. He fell asleep with his candle burning and the drapes caught fire. He managed to smother the flames before they spread too far. Lucky escape, eh? The whole house could have gone up. Did the commotion not wake you? Did you hear nothing?"

"I did," I replied, then lowered my voice so the other maids couldn't hear. "I thought it was Pilot. But Pilot cannot laugh."

"Laugh?" She smiled. "Oh, no ... you must have been dreaming, miss."

"I was not."

"Did you not look to see what was out there?" Grace asked.

"No ..." I said. "I bolted the door."

"Very wise, miss." Grace fixed me with a stare. "Might be an idea to do that every night. Thornfield is such an isolated spot. Who knows what ruffians might try to break in? Best to be on the safe side."

I knew this was some kind of threat. If I was troubled by last night's events, now I was doubly chilled. Questions plagued me, but Mr. Rochester had told me to say nothing. He trusted me, and I couldn't break that. I was more desperate than ever to talk to him. Surely he'd send for me soon?

He did not.

Afternoon gave way to evening and there was still no word from him. When Mary came to my door, it was only to tell me that my tea was in the parlor.

Mrs. Fairfax was filling the pot when she said, "What fine weather we've had. It was a pleasant day for Mr. Rochester's journey."

Journey? He'd left Thornfield Hall? My heart sank like a stone.

Mrs. Fairfax told me he'd gone to some grand party at a mansion ten miles or more away. He wasn't expected home for a week or more. There were ladies there, she said, and one that Mr. Rochester was especially drawn to.

She was a rare beauty called Miss Blanche Ingram.

16.

You're a fool, Jane Eyre, I told my reflection. An idiot. You're a hired hand, a paid servant, and an ugly one at that! Look at you! You stupid, silly girl. Did you really think Mr. Rochester liked you? Did you really believe he found your company interesting? He was bored, that was all. He was an idle gentleman amusing himself with the nearest toy. And now he's gone off to play among the gentry, where he belongs.

It was only now that I realized how deep a hole I'd fallen in. Had Lowood taught me nothing? How had I let it happen? Love had crept up on me like a thief, so slowly and so silently I'd never seen it coming. And now Mr. Rochester had gone, and he'd carried my poor heart away with him.

A week passed. No word came.

Ten days. Still nothing.

Mrs. Fairfax thought Mr. Rochester would go on from the house party to London and then to France, maybe, or Italy. It was his way, she said. He might not come home for a year or more.

A year? It seemed like an eternity!

It took every morsel of willpower I had to hold myself together.

For the next few days I carried on from minute to minute and hour to hour as if nothing was wrong. Yet inside I was slowly bleeding to death.

But after two weeks a letter came for Mrs. Fairfax. The master was coming home in three days. He was bringing the gentlemen from the house party with him. And the ladies.

Such activity followed! It seemed that the rooms Mrs. Fairfax kept clean and ready in case of Mr. Rochester's arrival were nowhere near clean or ready enough for guests. The house was turned upside down. An army of servants was drafted in from the village, but it was still not enough. Adèle was in a frenzy of excitement, but even if she'd been able to concentrate there could be no lessons, for I was pressed into service in the kitchen.

I was kept so busy that thoughts of Grace Poole were pushed from my mind. Apart from one small instance. I was cracking eggs into a bowl for the cook when Grace came in for her usual pot of ale. After she'd gone, two of the kitchen maids started whispering about how much money Grace was paid, and how they wouldn't do her job, not for all the gold in Christendom. I edged closer so I could hear more, but they saw me. One maid said to the other, "Doesn't she know?" The second replied with a shake of the head.

It made me break out into a sweat. I was holding secrets for Mr. Rochester. But there was something going on that he was keeping from me.

17.

Mr. Rochester and the ladies and gentlemen were due to arrive at six that evening. They were late. It was closer to seven when word came that the party was on its way. Adèle and I watched for the arrival from a window.

The house had felt like a crypt. Then a home. Now it was transformed into a theater.

First, Mr. Rochester entered stage left, galloping down the drive on his great black stallion. Pilot ran ahead. And beside Mr. Rochester was a lady on a chestnut mare. She was dressed in purple silk, her skirt almost brushing the ground, her veil streaming out behind her. This was Miss Blanche Ingram making her entrance.

Not far behind them were two carriages crammed with gentlemen in fine suits and ladies in beautiful silk gowns.

I had never seen parrots, but Mr. Rochester had described them once: great flocks of brightly colored birds that squawked and screeched. Their noise and chatter filled the air so a person could not hear themselves think. I'd not been able to imagine it before. I could now.

Adèle and I were not called for that night. I hoped we'd not be summoned at all while the visitors were at Thornfield Hall. But the following evening Mrs. Fairfax told me Mr. Rochester had requested our presence. The thought of being in the guests' company made me shake, but Mrs. Fairfax reassured me. All Adèle and I needed to do, she said, was go into the drawing room before the ladies came away from the dinner table.

"Find a quiet corner and stay there until the gentlemen join the ladies," Mrs. Fairfax told me. "Let Mr. Rochester see you're there, then slip away. No one will notice."

I wore the gray dress I'd made for Miss Temple's wedding. I pinned the brooch she'd given me at my throat. Adèle wore her pink dress and satin slippers. Together we went into the drawing room. I sat in the window seat, a book open in my lap, but I couldn't read a word. Adèle sat beside me, overwhelmed and unusually silent.

The ladies made their grand entrance not long after. When she saw their bright dresses and sparkling jewels, Adèle could sit still no longer. The moment they were over the threshold she ran across the room and greeted them with a curtsy. They took her to the sofa and fussed over her as if she were a doll.

I watched Blanche Ingram carefully. She was indeed lovely to look at, but she was so proud of herself! She seemed to think she'd created her face and body all on her own, not been gifted them by God. When she noticed me, her nostrils flared. A look of distaste curled her lip as if I were something nasty Pilot had left behind. I realized then that Blanche Ingram's beauty went no deeper than her skin. Inside she was an ugly, ill-tempered witch.

My opinion of Miss Ingram was confirmed when the gentlemen came in. Mr. Rochester was last into the room. My heart was pounding so hard I thought he'd hear it, but he didn't even glance my way. He sat himself down beside Miss Ingram, and it wasn't long before their talk turned to Adèle and her education. Miss Ingram thought it highly amusing to tell tales of how she'd teased her own governesses and made their lives a misery. How useless we were as a breed, Miss Ingram said, and how ridiculous! Mr. Rochester made no attempt to defend me. He allowed every one of Miss Ingram's barbed remarks to hit its target. The man I thought I'd known was gone. Mr. Rochester had been replaced by a loud, laughing oaf.

I had never felt pain like it. I'd committed no sin, but I'd been cast out of paradise. I felt myself slipping through my own fingers. Where was Jane Eyre? Where was the rage that had carried me so reliably before now? It was gone. I felt no anger, only a deep, deep sadness.

Blanche Ingram was tired of talking. She moved to the piano, and Mr. Rochester, her devoted admirer, followed. I can get away now, I thought.

But then Mr. Rochester started singing, and there was something in his voice that skewered my heart and would not let me go.

The moment he'd finished, I slipped out of the side door. My eyes blurred with unshed tears. I paused to rub them away, and then I heard another door open and Mr. Rochester was before me.

"How are you?" he asked.

I had to scrape together all my courage to answer calmly, "I'm well."

"Why didn't you come and speak to me?"

I bit back a sharp retort and instead said, "You seemed busy. I didn't wish to disturb you."

"You're pale," Mr. Rochester told me. "What's the matter?"

"Nothing."

"Did you catch a cold the night you tried to drown me?"

"No," I said.

"Come back inside. It's still early."

"I'm tired, sir."

"And depressed," he said. "You're so depressed that a few more words would make your tears flow freely. If I didn't dread the servants' gossip, I'd demand to know why. Tonight, I excuse you. But while my visitors are here I expect you in the drawing room every evening. Good night, my . . ."

Mr. Rochester stopped, bit his lip, and left me.

What in the devil's name was the man playing at?

18.

The house party at Thornfield Hall showed no sign of ever coming to an end. You couldn't move without falling over ladies' maids and gentlemen's valets. The kitchens never ceased turning out food to satisfy the crowd. While the servants worked their fingers to the bone, the gentlemen and ladies romped and played like overgrown children. At their center stood Mr. Rochester, like a puppet master with his marionettes. And always at his side was Miss Blanche Ingram, laughing, clapping, cheering him on.

It was common knowledge Mr. Rochester planned to marry her. I loved him. I couldn't just stop, much as I wanted to. Days extended to weeks, and I was in constant, unrelenting agony.

Maybe if Blanche Ingram had been brilliantly witty or extremely clever or very kind I'd have minded less. But she was none of those things. She was self-centered, self-satisfied, so in love with her own reflection she hardly needed a suitor. She hated every bone in my body and was spiteful to Adèle—a seven-year-old child—who only ever tried to please her.

And was Mr. Rochester so madly in love, so dazzled by her beauty, that he didn't understand her true nature?

No!

He saw Miss Ingram's faults as clearly as I did. I'd catch him looking at her, a flicker of distaste passing across his features. He did not love her. And yet she was destined to be his wife. Why? Wealth, I supposed. Beauty. Family connections. Power. I don't know. The rich and powerful move in mysterious ways.

Mr. Rochester was the heart and life and soul of the party. When business called him away from the house, a dreary dullness crept over Thornfield Hall like a thick fog.

One morning he'd gone to the village and was not likely to return until after dark. It was raining sideways, so the walk his guests had planned—to look at the wild gypsies who were camped on the common—was postponed. Instead, the men whiled away the day playing pool, the women cards.

Mr. Rochester might have been away, but the order that Adèle and I go to the drawing room in the evening hadn't changed. When the gentlemen and ladies came in that night, I was surprised to see a stranger among them. I gathered from listening that he was an old friend of the master's who'd arrived from overseas. His name was Mr. Mason.

The dullness of the evening was broken when a footman brought word that an old gypsy woman had come to the house. She was sitting in the library asking to read the young ladies' palms.

A fortune-teller! An air of excitement rippled around the room. The men wanted the gypsy thrown out, but fearless Miss Ingram was in a mood to be entertained. She swept out of the drawing room, head held high, confident that her fortune held nothing but delight.

Whatever Miss Ingram was told, she didn't like it. She was back only a few minutes later, her lovely face creased into an ugly frown.

The other ladies had a happier time. One by one, they disappeared nervously and then returned to the drawing room flushed, saying, "She knows so much! She said such things! It was uncanny!"

I stayed in my place, but then the footman was tugging at my sleeve. He whispered in my ear that the gypsy said there was another lady in the room. She wouldn't leave until she'd seen the small, plain one who occupied the window seat.

19.

The old gypsy sat hunched in a chair in the library, wrapped in a cloak, wearing a hat that threw a shadow over her face. She smelled of smoke and damp earth and the wild outdoors.

"And so she comes," the fortune-teller said in a cracked, rasping voice. "The little one that tucks herself away in the window seat and prays not to be seen. But my seer's eye found you. Why don't you tremble?"

"I'm not cold," I said.

"Why aren't you pale?"

"I'm not sick."

The gypsy leaned forward. "Why aren't you scared of my fortune-teller's art?"

"I'm not silly," I told her.

She laughed, a wheeze that ended in a cough. Pulling a pipe from the folds of her cloak, she lit it and smoked for a while. Then she said very slowly and clearly, "You are cold, you are sick, you are silly."

"Why?" I asked. "Because I don't believe in your seer's eye? You got your information from the servants."

The gypsy pointed a dirty finger at my chest. "You are cold because you will not let that fire burn. You are sick because you will not admit your feelings. You are silly because happiness is right in front of you and you cannot see it." She put the pipe back to her lips and added, "You are a young woman. Unmarried. Is there a gentleman in this house your heart yearns for?"

"No," I said.

"What of the master?"

"He's not home."

"An evasive answer! My sight tells me he's to be married—"

"The servants have told you that too," I said, cutting her short. "I didn't come to hear his fortune. You're supposed to be telling me mine."

The gypsy wouldn't read my palm. She said she'd tell my fortune from my face. I was told to kneel by the fire so she could examine me, and I obliged. I had nothing better to do.

She put her hand under my chin, her palm against my throat. I'd doubted her power, but the moment her skin touched mine I felt something thrillingly strange happening. She'd thrown me into a kind of bewitched dream. The gypsy traced my features with her fingers, and her light touch set every nerve in my body burning. Honey seemed to be flowing through my veins. I stopped resisting.

She began to speak—words that were a beautiful, magical riddle.

"What have we here?" the gypsy said. "A fire that burns inside. I see it in eyes so soft, so full of feeling. But oh! Such sad and lonely eyes. These eyes speak of a mighty yearning. A powerful pain. These eyes speak of a heart that is breaking."

The fortune-teller's finger passed across my lips as she continued, "This mouth delights in laughter. It is a mouth that should speak freely and smile often and be silenced only with a kiss. But this mouth is sealed. It must obey custom and tradition. It must be polite and courteous and humble. It must express only gratitude and will not spill the words it longs to."

She ran her fingers over my forehead. "This brow declares the mouth will not speak. This brow declares it must not. This brow tells me of a lifetime's restraint, a lifetime's self-control, a lifetime's knowing her place. And so reason will rule passion, reason will prevent her falling into an abyss of desire. Tempests may blow and earthquakes may shake, but she will remain in possession of herself. Nothing will break through. Well said, brow. You have been honest. Your declaration shall be respected. For now."

The gypsy took my face in both hands. Her face hovered above mine, her eyes so close I felt I was falling into them. And now her voice changed as she said, "I want this moment to last forever, but it must stop. Get up, Miss Eyre. The play is over."

The enchantment was broken. I got to my feet, my heart thumping, my hands shaking. The gypsy was pulling off her cloak. Her hat. And there stood my master.

"Mr. Rochester!" I gasped. I didn't know what else to say. "What a trick to play!"

"Something to pass the time," he said. "Well carried out, don't you think? The other ladies were taken in. The things they told me! But you gave nothing away. You were very correct. Very sensible."

"May I go now?"

"No . . ." he said, and put a hand on my arm. "What have they been doing in the drawing room?"

"Discussing the gypsy, mostly. Oh—did you know a stranger has arrived? He said he's an old friend of yours. Mr. Mason?"

Mr. Rochester's hand shook. The smile froze on his lips. Breath left his chest. He sat down.

"Are you ill?" I asked.

"Jane . . . oh, Jane . . . my dearest friend . . . this is a blow," he said at last. "A bitter blow indeed. Oh, God, he'll kill me!"

"What can I do?"

Mr. Rochester sent me to the dining room for a glass of wine. And after I'd brought it and after he'd swallowed it down, he sent me back to Mr. Mason. I whispered into his ear that Mr. Rochester was home and waiting for him in the library. And then I went to bed like he'd told me to.

But I could not rest until I heard the guests retiring to their rooms. Mr. Rochester's voice rose above the others, saying, "This way, Mason. Here's your chamber."

Whatever Mr. Rochester had dreaded hadn't happened. He sounded cheerful. Relaxed. I settled down to sleep.

20.

A scream jerked me from my sleep. The sound was so savage, so raw, I was out of my bed before I knew I was awake.

I hadn't drawn my curtains. A full moon flooded my room with light. There was a moment's hush, and then directly above my head I heard a muffled voice beg, "Help! Help! Rochester!"

There was the creak of a door opening. Heavy feet ran along the corridor and up the stairs. Something thudded above my head.

Then more doors banged open. Guests tumbled from their rooms, clucking like frightened chickens:

"Is it a fire?"

"Robbers?"

"Thieves?"

And, "Where the devil is Rochester?"

"Here!" Mr. Rochester called, coming back along the corridor carrying a candle and looking perfectly composed.

The ladies flocked to him, Miss Ingram clinging around his neck as if she might faint. Mr. Rochester told them the scream had come from a maid who was having a nightmare. It took him some time to soothe his guests, but one by one they returned to their rooms. As did I.

But not to sleep.

I dressed in silence. And when the house was sleeping once more there came a knock on my door.

"Am I wanted, sir?" I asked.

"Yes," Mr. Rochester replied.

I unbolted my door.

"Have you a sponge?" he asked. "Smelling salts?"

"Both."

"Bring them."

I followed where he led me. We padded along the corridor, soft-footed as cats, then up the stairs to the third floor. Mr. Rochester paused outside the room I'd first seen Grace Poole emerge from.

"You don't faint at the sight of blood, do you?" he asked.

"I don't think so," I said.

After unlocking the door, we entered and I saw the tapestry on the far wall was rumpled. It had been pulled back to reveal a second, hidden door.

A snarling noise was coming from a room that lay beyond. It was almost canine, but no living dog sounded like that. It was followed by Grace Poole's joyless, demonic laughter.

Mr. Mason was slumped in the single chair. I thought he was sleeping until Mr. Rochester carried the candle nearer. One arm of Mr. Mason's shirt was scarlet.

I was to bathe his arm, to wash away the blood, to keep him awake with smelling salts while my master rode for the doctor. Before Mr. Rochester left he told Mr. Mason he was not to speak to me—not one word.

Then he was gone. And he locked the door behind us.

I had thought the red room bad. The night of the fire was worse. But this was beyond anything I could have imagined. Locked in a room with a man who was bleeding so heavily I thought he'd surely die. And only a door separating us from the woman who'd attacked him. Why was Grace Poole still here? What devil's bargain kept her protected? What in the name of God was going on?

I watched the candle burn lower and lower. I watched my patient get paler and paler. I watched the bowl of water get thicker and thicker with blood, and still I kept cleaning his wound. It was harder and harder to keep Mr. Mason conscious.

I listened for the chiming of the clock. One hour passed. Two.

The candle puttered and died. I would have despaired, but fingers of gray light were poking under the curtains. Dawn could not be far off. I heard Pilot bark. And not long after that Mr. Rochester was back with the doctor.

"Be quick," my master told him as they came into the room. "The sun will soon rise, and by then I must have Mason away for the sake of the creature in there." Mr. Rochester's head jerked toward the hidden door, and he added, "I've kept it quiet this long, I don't want it coming out now."

The doctor asked no questions. He bandaged his patient, only noting that the wounds were made both with a blade and with teeth.

"She bit me," said Mr. Mason. "She tore at me like a tigress when Rochester got the knife away. She sucked my blood. She said she'd drain my heart." He began to sob.

Perhaps to prevent me hearing more, I was sent running to fetch Mr. Mason's cloak. Then to find a vial of medicine from Mr. Rochester's room, and finally to tell the driver of the carriage waiting outside that the men would be down shortly.

The sun was rising when Mr. Rochester and the doctor loaded Mr. Mason into the carriage. Servants and guests still slept. Whatever the secret was, it remained undiscovered.

"Take care of her as best you can," Mr. Mason said to my master.

"I've done so all these years," Mr. Rochester replied. "I'll not stop now."

The carriage drove away.

So Mr. Mason did not hear my master, his friend, say under his breath, "I wish to God it was over."

21.

After the carriage had left, Mr. Rochester said to me, "Don't go back in. The house is like a prison. Come into the orchard. Breathe some fresh air."

The sky was threaded with reds and golds. A mist rose from the grass. I wouldn't have been surprised to see fairies flitting between the trees. It was an enchanted morning after a night of bloody horror.

"You ask me nothing," Mr. Rochester said. "Not a question, not a look, not even a raised eyebrow."

"Your secrets are yours to keep or tell as you see fit, sir," I replied.

"That's a servant's answer. Hired hands must do as they are told, mustn't they? If I commanded you to the gates of hell, you'd feel obliged to pack your bags and go. Yet you seem to do my bidding willingly. You never drag your feet. Is that because I'm your master or because you're my most true and loyal friend? Can friendship really exist between master and servant? Or does the difference in status make it impossible, I wonder? Do you consider me your friend, Jane?"

How was I to answer? I'd thought of Mr. Rochester as a friend once, but would a friend see me mocked by Miss Ingram and do nothing? Yet, wounded as I was, I knew I'd lay my life down for him if he asked.

"I do your bidding because my heart tells me to," I said.

"A friend's answer!" he declared. "Good."

Mr. Rochester settled on a bench and told me to sit down next to him.

"Then let me ask you something," he said. "As a friend. A purely hypothetical question. Suppose there was a young man. Rich. Spoiled. Living a wild life in a foreign land. Suppose he committed a terrible error—an error, not a sin—and the consequences followed him for his whole life. He tried to wipe that error from his mind by losing himself in wine and women, but he found that nothing—nothing!—worked. Nothing could drive the poison from his brain. Suppose the man returned home older and wiser, but a weary, withered soul. Then he found a stranger waiting for him. A stranger who possessed every quality he'd searched for all those years. Wit, intelligence, sense, a quick and inquiring mind, a true and noble heart. The stranger could wipe away the error and drive out the poison. The stranger could save this man's troubled soul. Would he be justified in overcoming every obstacle to take that prize?"

I had no idea what to say. Once more Mr. Rochester was talking in riddles. Once more I found myself quoting Helen Burns. "Salvation can't be found in our fellow creatures. We must look to God, not man."

"But suppose it was God's will?" Mr. Rochester asked. "Suppose God sent the stranger to him? Suppose the stranger is God's instrument?"

His look was so intense I felt myself slipping, spinning out of control. Dropping my eyes, I sat perfectly still.

"I've been a reckless, foolish man, Jane," Mr. Rochester said. "But I believe I've found my salvation in ..."

He stopped. The silence drew out like a thread and then suddenly snapped. Mr. Rochester's mood changed. The softness vanished and a note of harsh sarcasm entered his voice.

"Miss Ingram. She will save me. She'll save me with a vengeance. Go to bed, Jane. Get some sleep."

22.

The night after Mr. Mason's hasty departure, I had another strange dream. I'd been troubled by them for a week or more. They all involved the same small child. Sometimes I hushed them to sleep in my arms. Sometimes the child played on the lawn among the daisies or dabbled their hands in the stream. At other times they ran away from me and I couldn't find them. This particular night, the child wailed endlessly and I could do nothing to comfort them.

The following morning I got word that my aunt had sent for me. It seemed my cousin John had drunk and gambled his mother's money away and then killed himself. The shock had nearly killed my aunt too. She hadn't long to live, the message said, and was asking for me.

I needed permission to leave my place of employment. I went in search of Mr. Rochester and found him playing pool with Miss Ingram. The expression on her face when I interrupted them was so sour it could have turned wine into vinegar.

Mr. Rochester reluctantly gave me leave to go. Before I departed I begged a favor of him. I made him promise that Adèle would be safely in school and I would be safely in a new place before he married his bride.

I'd vowed never to set foot in Gateshead again, yet the next morning I was on my way there.

It was a long, weary journey, more than a hundred miles of being jolted and jarred over rough roads. And when I arrived there was no tearful reunion. No deathbed reconciliation. My aunt did not ask for my forgiveness, so I did not give it. She was raving most of the time. She repeated my name over and over. "Jane Eyre ... Jane Eyre ... Where's Jane Eyre?" But in between she also said, "Horrid ... nasty ... demon ... devil." My aunt only recognized me once, when she stared into my face with such violent dislike it made her shudder from head to toe.

It's a strange thing. With some folk there's a connection made on the first meeting—sometimes, even before a word is spoken, a friendship blossoms. But if there are sympathetic souls that attract each other, then there must also be those that repel.

I had no hatred for my aunt, not anymore. Helen Burns had talked it out of me long ago. Hatred is a strange poison, Helen had told me. It is utterly harmless to the hated person. It only kills the one who allows hate to grow and fester within them. I had let my feelings wither and die, but my aunt clung to hers like a life raft. Even on her deathbed she would not, could not, let her hatred go. For it would mean admitting she was wrong about me, and her pride was greater than her need for forgiveness.

My aunt lasted only a week after my arrival. There's a great deal to do after somebody dies, and my cousins were not used to work. I made all the necessary arrangements, I wrote all the necessary letters, I performed all the necessary duties. I'd told Mr. Rochester I'd be gone a week. But it was closer to a month before I returned to Thornfield Hall.

23.

Gateshead had housed me for the first ten miserable years of my life. I'd been happier at Lowood, but a charitable institution is not a home.

I felt like a swallow as I returned to Thornfield, coming back to its nest after a long time in a foreign land. I longed to see the gardens, to walk in the orchard, to glimpse the wild moor beyond.

Most of all, I longed to see Mr. Rochester.

Knowing everything would be ripped away from me brought me close to tears. Soon I'd be in a new place with a new master, maybe teaching pupils as spoiled and ignorant as Miss Ingram. When the coach pulled up to the village, I didn't send for the carriage to take me back to Thornfield Hall. My emotions were running so high that I decided to walk there in solitude.

I thought I was in control of my feelings until I rounded the corner in the lane and there was Mr.

Rochester, on the steps where I'd once sat myself. Every nerve in me was suddenly unstrung.

"Jane Eyre!" he called. "Where the devil have you been this last month?"

"With my aunt, who is dead," I replied.

He laughed. "So you do come from the spirit world. I knew you were not human! You've been with the angels all this time, have you? Absent from home a whole month and forgetting my existence, no doubt."

Home. He'd called Thornfield my home. I was suddenly brimming with happiness. Mr. Rochester stood aside so I could climb the steps over the wall and cut across the fields. Once I'd reached the other side a strange impulse made me spin back round to face him.

"Thank you, Mr. Rochester, for your great kindness," I said. "I'm so glad to get back to you. Wherever you are is my home."

I walked away so fast he couldn't have caught up with me, not even if he'd been galloping on his horse.

Adèle was overjoyed when she saw me. Mrs. Fairfax greeted me with a warm embrace, Mary and the other maids with smiles. I was at home. And now I was with what felt like family.

I shut my eyes against the future. I blocked my ears against the voice that warned me of the separation that would come. I sank into Thornfield Hall like a weary traveler into a warm bath.

Two weeks followed that were strangely calm. Nothing was said of the master's marriage. No preparations were made, no date was set, and there were no journeys back and forward between the lovers. Miss Ingram did not come to the hall, and Mr. Rochester did not visit Miss Ingram. If the match had been called off, he was surprisingly cheerful about it. Mr. Rochester had never called for me so often and never been kinder when I was in his presence. It was harder and harder to remember who and what I was. I had to remind myself of it nightly, staring at my reflection. *You are plain Jane Eyre*, I told myself. *A nothing. A nobody. Stop this nonsense!*

It didn't work. I was more helplessly and hopelessly in love with him than ever.

24.

It was midsummer's eve. Adèle had tired herself out gathering wild strawberries in the lane and had gone to bed with the sun. I slipped out of the house and into the garden. The moon was rising. A nightingale sang in the woods.

Mr. Rochester was outside too, enjoying the cool of the day. I tried to turn away before he could see me, but I was too late.

"Jane!" he called. "Walk with me."

I felt uneasy being out alone with him, and so late, but I could find no excuse for leaving his side.

Mr. Rochester spoke of Thornfield—what a pleasant place it was and how I must be fond of it and its inhabitants? I agreed I was.

We came to the great horse chestnut tree. He stopped and leaned his back against it.

For a moment or two I was perfectly happy. And then he killed me with his words.

"You will be sorry to leave, I know," Mr. Rochester said. "And yet you must go."

He was to be married, he told me, to his beautiful Blanche. He'd found a school for Adèle. And he'd got me a new place with a family in Ireland.

Ireland! A distant land, across the sea, so very, very far away from him! I would never see Mr. Rochester again. Never! I must not cry. I must not let him see my distress, but an ache in my chest made me struggle for breath. I felt as if my heart would burst through my ribs.

I tried to listen, but it took several moments before I realized he was speaking not of Blanche but of me. "It's a curious thing ... this friendship of ours ... It's almost as if a string ties us. I can feel it knotted here in my chest. I have the strangest fear that when you go, that string will snap and I will bleed to death. But I'm being ridiculous. You'd forget me soon enough."

"Never!" I replied. I could say no more. I folded my arms, clutched myself tight together.

The nightingale sang louder, and that sweet song pierced my pain. All my restraint, all my self-control suddenly slipped between my fingers.

I wept. Tears poured from my eyes. And words so long held in spilled from my mouth.

"It will kill me to go," I said. "I love Thornfield, not because it's grand or splendid but because I've *lived* here. Truly lived. And loved. My soul has been fed. My heart and mind have soared to the heavens and beyond. It's been your doing, Mr. Rochester. I've seen what's bright and beautiful and glorious, and now it must be snatched away. I know I need to go. But looking at the future is like looking into my own grave."

"Why do you need to go?" he asked.

"Because of your bride!"

"I have none."

"But you will."

Mr. Rochester clenched his teeth. "I will," he said. "I will!"

My pain became a wild, unruly beast. "Then I must go," I went on. "Do you think I can stay here and be nothing to you? Do you think I'm a machine without feeling? Do you think because I'm poor and plain I'm soulless and heartless? You think wrong! I have as much soul as you and as much heart. And if God had given me beauty and wealth I'd have made it as hard for you to leave me as it is now for me to leave you. I'm not speaking as your servant. You're not my master anymore. My spirit is speaking directly to yours now as if we'd both passed through the grave and were standing at God's feet, equal—as we are!"

"As we are!" The words burst from him in a delighted cry. "As we are. Indeed, we are. I have waited so very, very long to hear you say that." Mr. Rochester tried to me pull into his arms.

But the rage that had made me speak still flooded my veins. "Let me go!" I said.

"Stop it!" he told me. "You're struggling like a trapped bird."

"I'm no bird. Nothing holds me. I'm a free human being with a free will, and when you marry I will leave you."

Mr. Rochester released me. "Your free will shall decide your future," he said. "Yours and yours alone. I'm offering you my hand, Jane, and my heart."

"You're laughing at me," I replied.

"Jane, Jane, Jane ... it's you I hope to marry. Come to me, Jane. Please."

Still I thought he mocked me. "Your bride stands between us," I said.

"My bride is here," he said, taking my hand. "I love you as my own flesh."

"Then what the devil have you been playing at with Miss Ingram all this time?" I demanded.

Mr. Rochester had the grace to look ashamed. "Forgive me. You and I are twin souls, Jane. Equals. But the world doesn't see it that way. I'm your master, but I can't command you to love me. I don't want you to feel obliged to marry me—I want you to do it of your own free will. I want *you* to choose *me*. I had to drive you into a fury that overcame reason, that overcame restraint, that washed all ideas of rank and wealth and servitude from your mind. You claimed me as your equal just now. *You* claimed *me*. Would you have dared do that if I hadn't driven you to such extremes of passion?"

"It was unkind."

"It was necessary."

"To break Miss Ingram's heart?" I said.

"Oh, Jane, she has no heart to break." He laughed. "When she heard a rumor that I was not as wealthy as I seemed, her passion cooled in a heartbeat."

"A rumor spread by you, no doubt."

"I'm afraid so," Mr. Rochester admitted. "Can you forgive me?"

I was bewildered. "I can hardly believe it," I said. "You truly want me to be your wife?"

"I swear it."

"Then, yes. Yes! I will marry you."

My wild sadness was swept aside by an equally wild, delighted joy. My heart was so full I thought it would burst. Tears ran down my face, and the more Mr. Rochester kissed them away the more they flowed. He wrapped his arms around me, and we clung together so tight I thought we would melt into one flesh.

"Let no man meddle," Mr. Rochester said. "I will have her, and I will hold her. She was friendless, and I found her. I will cherish her as she deserves, and God will not judge me. He will not!"

I should have wondered what his words meant, but I was so consumed and so dazed with passion I did not ask.

We didn't notice the clouds rolling across the sky, blotting out the moon. We paid no heed to the great horse chestnut tree that now bent and groaned as the wind shook it. It was only when a bolt of lightning ripped across the sky and a clap of thunder made the ground shake beneath our feet that we realized a storm had broken.

We ran back to the house in pelting rain. And there in the hallway Mr. Rochester kissed me again and again. It was late, very late, before we let each other go.

The following morning, Adèle came running into my room to tell me that the great horse chestnut tree had been struck by lightning during the night.

It was split in two.

25.

In one month's time, plain Jane Eyre was to be married. I could hardly believe it.

Mr. Rochester was a rich man. He wanted to demonstrate his love the only way he knew how—by pouring jewels into my lap, by dressing me up like a doll in bright silks with frills and ruffles and satin slippers to match. He wanted to buy me bonnets with ostrich feathers the length of my arm.

I would have none of it. I was no Cécile Varens. Plain Jane Eyre, dressed in finery? No! I'd look like an organ grinder's monkey. Absurd. Ridiculous. I would not have known myself.

Mr. Rochester wanted to spend those four short weeks of courtship doing nothing but gazing into each other's eyes. I'd have none of that either. I refused to change my routine. I carried on spending my days with Adèle in the schoolroom. I came to the library with her in the evenings after Mr. Rochester had eaten. And while we were there

I wouldn't let him play the part of the besotted lover. I did not want silly talk or adoration. I wanted conversation. Debate. I provoked him, I teased, I irritated my future husband back into some sort of sense.

I did a better job with him than I did with myself. He'd become heaven and earth to me. For all his talk of us being equals I was consumed by him. After a month, there seemed to be nothing left of me at all.

26.

Four short weeks of courtship slipped away. Suddenly, it was the eve of our wedding. In the morning, I would be married. Afterward I'd be carried away from my makeshift family at Thornfield and into the unknown. Mr. Rochester was taking me to London and then Paris, Rome, Vienna. The trunks were already packed and standing in the hall, bearing labels that said "Mrs. Rochester." Who was she? I wondered. A stranger, not yet born.

I couldn't calm myself that last day. The night before, I'd been troubled by dreams that were so odd, so vivid, that even in the daylight I couldn't tell what was real and what was not.

My beloved had been called away on business, and I waited and watched for his return with increasing anxiety. As darkness fell I could stay still no longer. I went out, running along the lane to meet him.

I'd not gone far before I heard the sound of hooves. There he was, stretching his hand out, pulling me up onto the horse in front of him. Wrapping his cloak around me, Mr. Rochester kissed me long and hard, and then asked, "Why did you come out in the dark? Is there something wrong?"

It was not until we were both sitting by the library fire that I told him what had so unsettled me. That I'd dreamed I was walking a long, lonely road carrying a child in my arms. They whimpered and would not be comforted. My beloved was riding away from me, and I could not catch up to him. And then I'd come over the crest of a hill and there was Thornfield Hall. For a moment I'd thought I was home and safe. But then the clouds peeled away from the moon and I saw it was a crumbling ruin, haunted by bats.

It had been such a ghastly vision that I'd woken up, or so I thought.

There was a candle burning in my room, and I saw a woman looking at my wedding dress. It was not Mrs. Fairfax, it was not Mary. I didn't know her. She was shrouded in white like a ghost, and then she picked up my veil and threw it over her head. When she looked in the mirror, I could see her reflection. A horrible face. Bloodshot eyes, swollen lips. She looked like a vampire. Suddenly she ripped the veil from her head and tore at it with her teeth. And then she came to the bed and held the candle right up to my face. I felt her hot, sour breath on my skin. And, for the second time in my life, pure terror made me faint.

"When I woke, it was daylight," I told Mr. Rochester. "And my veil was lying on the floor, ripped in two. Now tell me who and what that creature was."

He shuddered, pulling me close, whether for my comfort or his I couldn't tell. It was some minutes before my beloved said, "I know what must have happened. Someone came to your room. Grace Poole most likely. But you were still half asleep. Your dreaming mind made a phantom of her. I know you've wondered why I keep her here. After we're married I'll tell you, but not now."

His explanation seemed good enough, and I could come up with nothing better. It was well past midnight: time for us to part.

"Don't sleep in your own bed tonight," Mr. Rochester said. "Go to Adèle's. You're anxious, my love. You should have company."

I did as he suggested, bolting Adèle's door behind me. For what remained of the night Adèle slept sweetly in my arms, but I did not sleep at all.

27.

I was dressed as a bride. When I looked at my reflection, I saw a stranger.

A wedding day should be enchanting and delightful, should it not? Every moment is to be relished.

But when I went down the stairs, my beloved was pacing the hallway. Mr. Rochester was on fire with impatience to get the ceremony over. Horses were hitched to the carriage, and it stood outside, ready and waiting to carry us off to London before we'd even walked to church. There was no time for breakfast. Mr. Rochester held my hand in a tight grip and strode so fast I could barely keep up. And his face! There was no joy in it. No softness. Not a trace of love. Never did a bridegroom look so grimly determined. It was as if he were leading me into battle. By the time we reached the church gate, I was gasping for breath.

Mr. Rochester paused for a moment then. I noticed a stranger standing in the corner among the gravestones. He slipped away out of sight before I had breath enough to point him out.

I was marched up the path and into the church. We stood at the altar, Mr. Rochester's back stiff. One of his hands still clutched mine, the other was clenched into a fist.

The ceremony began.

I heard a step behind me, and I turned my head. The stranger had slid into a pew at the back of the church.

The vicar was speaking. "If either of you know any impediment why you may not lawfully be joined together in matrimony, you must now confess it."

He paused but clearly didn't expect anyone to interrupt the silence. The vicar didn't even lift his eyes from the prayer book. It was when he turned to ask my beloved, "Will thou have this woman ...?" that the stranger's voice rang out.

"I declare an impediment," he said.

My beloved didn't move. "Go on," Mr. Rochester growled at the vicar. "Hurry."

"I can't ..." the vicar began.

"Mr. Rochester already has a wife," the stranger said. "She is alive and well and living at Thornfield Hall."

The vicar was stunned. "Impossible!" he declared. "I've lived here for years—I've never heard of a Mrs. Rochester."

"No, by God!" Mr. Rochester said. A grim smile twisted my beloved's face into something I barely recognized. "I took great care no one would know her by that name."

The stranger came toward us, and I realized it was Mr. Mason.

"Can you prove this?" asked the vicar.

"I can," Mr. Mason said. "I have the wedding certificate here. I'm her brother."

Mr. Rochester's head dropped to his chest. He was a man defeated. "The game is up," he said. "The play is done. The curtain falls. There will be no wedding today." Mr. Rochester lifted his chin and looked at the vicar. "You may not have heard of Mrs. Rochester, but you'll have heard the whispers about a mysterious person in the attic kept under lock and key. Some say she's my bastard sister. Others my cast-off mistress. No ... that person is my wife. I was cheated into marrying her fifteen years ago when she was a beauty and I was young and foolish and took what men said at their word. She is troubled, as her mother was before her. Her father and her brother kept this fact from me until after the wedding they had so hastily arranged. This girl," Mr. Rochester said, tugging my hand, "knew nothing of any of this. She is completely innocent. Come, all of you. Come and meet my wife."

He held me fast, pulling me out of the church and back to Thornfield Hall where the carriage was ready. Mrs. Fairfax and Adèle stood on the step waiting to bid us farewell.

"Take the carriage back to the coach house," Mr. Rochester told the driver. "Mrs. Fairfax, get Adèle out of my sight."

He strode up the stairs to the third floor, to the room with the second, hidden door. Yanking aside the tapestry, he opened it.

There inside the second, hidden room was Grace Poole.

And another person, who crouched in the corner on all fours, a mane of grizzled hair covering her face. She stood, rearing on her feet, and I recognized the bloodshot eyes, the swollen lips, the bloated features. It was my nightmare visitor.

When she saw Mr. Rochester, she sprang.

He threw me behind him as she seized him by the throat. Teeth snapped as she tried to bite. Mr. Rochester was a powerful man and could have brought her down with one blow, but he would not hurt her no matter how hard she tried to wound him. At last he pinned her arms behind her back and Grace tied them. Together they bound her to a chair while she snapped and growled.

"That," Mr. Rochester said, "is my wife." He laid a hand on my shoulder. "And this young girl, who stands so grave and quiet though I have dragged her to the mouth of hell, is who I longed to have and hold. Can you blame me?"

I shut myself in my room, bolting the door behind me.

I felt nothing. Not horror, not misery, not grief. Nothing.

I took off my wedding dress and put on my plain black gown. I sat down. I was so weak, so tired. I leaned my arms on the table and my head dropped down on them.

What had happened? I was not cut or bruised. My body was whole. And yet where was I? Jane Eyre was lost. Gone. I'd melted away like a wisp of smoke.

28.

It was late afternoon before I raised my head from the table.

I hadn't eaten or drunk that day. And no one had bothered me. There had been no knock on the door, no soft voice asking how I fared. Not even Adèle had come to find me. Did none of them care?

I drew back the bolt, opened the door, and stumbled over something.

Mr. Rochester was sitting outside.

"At last," he said. His voice was cracked with misery. "I've been here such a long time. You shut yourself up and you grieve alone. But not a sound, not a sob, not a cry has come from you. Has your heart been weeping blood? I never meant to wound you, Jane. Will you ever forgive me?"

I said nothing. I could not. I was chilled and tired and sick and close to fainting. Mr. Rochester carried me downstairs, placed me in a chair by the fire, and lifted a glass of wine to my lips.

Little by little, some sort of feeling returned to me. I wished I'd remained numb, for feeling was agony.

That afternoon and evening was an unbearable torment for both of us.

Mr. Rochester told me the long, sorry tale of a hasty marriage to a virtual stranger. He described his ghastly despair as he watched a debauched drunk of a wife sink into fits. He'd spent years running away, losing himself in wine and women, and returned home weary of the world and heartsore. Then he'd seen me sitting on the steps.

He begged me to go away with him. We could live in France, Mr. Rochester said, where we were not known. He would call himself my husband. I would be his wife in all but name.

"Will you not do it, Jane?" he asked. "Do you not love me enough?"

"Your marriage was an error," I said. "But this would be a sin. I love you too much to be the cause of your damnation."

Mr. Rochester would not give up. He painted such a picture of our future together! I was so sorely tempted. A voice at the back of my head whispered, You're a nothing. A nobody. Who will care what you do?

But a stronger voice—the voice of plain Jane Eyre who had survived the terrors of Gateshead and Lowood and Thornfield—replied, I care for myself. The more alone and friendless I am, the more I will respect myself. I cannot live a lie. I will not live in shame.

"Come with me," Mr. Rochester said. "You only have to say it, Jane. Say it now. 'I will be yours, Mr. Rochester.'"

"Mr. Rochester . . . I will not be yours."

"You can't mean for me to go one way in this world and you the other?"

"I can. And I do."

"Jane! You are my hope, my love, my life, my soul!" He started to sob as I walked away. "I cannot live without you. I cannot!"

I had reached the door but turned back. I kissed his cheek, I smoothed his hair.

"God bless you for your kindness," I said. "God keep you safe."

I left the room.

I rose before dawn. I took my purse, pinned on my shawl, tied my straw bonnet to my head, and slipped from Thornfield Hall before anyone else was up.

I loved Mr. Rochester so very, very much. One day more and he would have persuaded me to go with him. If I did that, I would lose myself forever. And then what would there have been for him to have loved back?

I walked to the village. I took the first coach, giving the driver every last coin I had to take me as far from Thornfield Hall as he could carry me.

And as the coach rattled along the lanes, I wept. And wept. And wept.

29.

A respectable woman can become a vagrant in a matter of days. She becomes hungry, dirty, and disheveled without a roof over her head, without a bed to sleep in, without regular meals, without money in her purse. She becomes a beggar. And then she becomes invisible.

I knocked on doors. No one would give me work.

I asked for scraps. I was not given them.

I would have starved. I was very close to it.

One evening, when night had started to fall and brought with it a whisper of autumn chill, I came to a wild expanse of moor. I was utterly lost and dizzy with fever. But in the distance was a house with a candle burning in the window. That flame drew me like a moth. I'd ask for food there, I thought. If they didn't give it to me, I'd lie down in a ditch and wait for death to take me.

But God had steered my footsteps to folk who were truly charitable. The house was occupied by a young clergyman and his two sisters. I was taken in. Fed. Bathed. Given clean clothes and cared for until I had recovered my health and strength.

I'll not say much about the time I spent with them. Only that I earned my keep working as a teacher in the village school.

Months passed. My heart did not heal. I lived, I worked, I walked and talked. Outwardly I looked whole. But I felt like a shadow with no substance. I'd left my soul at Thornfield Hall.

The clergyman was young and handsome and exceedingly godly.

One day he declared he was to be a missionary. We should marry, he informed me, not because he was in love but because I was plain and hardworking. I was created by God to serve others.

I considered accepting his offer. I was tired of struggling, tired of suffering. If hard work in a foreign land among the starving and diseased killed me, what of it? I was turning into Helen Burns at last: my eyes were fixed on the next life, not this one.

The clergyman pestered me about his offer for days. He wore away at my resistance until one evening when we stood in the garden I was on the brink of saying yes.

And then the strangest thing in my long, strange tale occurred. God tore a hole in the night sky and a despairing voice shouted through it. A voice I knew and loved so well called my name, "Jane! Jane! Jane!"

I ran forward but could see nothing.

"Where are you?" I called to Mr. Rochester. "Where are you?" No reply. "I'm coming," I yelled. "Wait!"

# 30.

And so, a full year after I'd run away, I returned home to Thornfield Hall.

I longed to sprout wings and fly, but I was a creature of earth, not heaven after all. I had to trundle along in a coach down roads and country lanes for mile after mile after mile. I slept one night in a tavern and the next day on I went again. In the afternoon, the landscape grew familiar. We had not yet reached the village when I called for the driver to stop. I could see a path, and if I was not mistaken it ran straight to the house.

I paid the driver, and I hurried across the fields.

My heart was overflowing with joy.

But when I reached the peak of the hill, horror sucked all the breath from my lungs.

Thornfield Hall was a burnt shell. A ruin.

*

I learned what had happened at a roadside inn.

A fire had broken out in the dead of night: always the time for calamities at the hall. I could guess who'd started it, but I let the innkeeper tell his tale as if to a stranger.

There was a woman kept in the attic, he said. She had been whispered of for years, but no one had ever seen her. Then there was a terrible scandal. The master of the house had wished to marry his governess—a small, ugly thing, folk said, but he was quite giddy with love for her. He took her to the church to be wed, but it turned out he was already married. The woman was the master's wife.

The nurse being paid to look after the woman was something of a drunk. The night of the fire she was fast asleep and snoring when the woman stole the keys from her belt.

The woman went looking for the governess and set a blaze burning in her room, but the governess had run away two months before. The master had been wild with grief. He'd sent his housekeeper away—paid her well, mind, but sent her off. And the little girl whom the governess had been teaching was sent to school. The master had shut himself away like a hermit and would see no one. So he was at home when the fire started, and he had no thought for his own safety. He got all the servants out—even the drunken nurse—but the woman went running up to the roof. She stood up there raving, and the master tried to get her back down. But she leaped at his throat, missed her footing, and fell, cracking her skull and spilling her brains upon the ground.

And the master? He survived, but only just. He was coming back down the main staircase when a beam collapsed on top of him. His right hand was crushed and had to be amputated. One of his eyes was gouged out, the other damaged so badly he could not see.

Injured, blinded: it would have been better if the poor man had died, the innkeeper told me.

I could not agree.

I asked where Mr. Rochester now lived. And then I begged the innkeeper to find a coach and driver who would take me there before nightfall.

31.

The light was fading when I walked toward the house.

Mary was setting Mr. Rochester's tea upon a tray when I arrived. She looked at me as if she were seeing a ghost. And then she embraced me so warmly it brought tears to my eyes.

"Will you tell him he has a visitor?" I said.

"He'll refuse," Mary replied. "He won't see anyone."

"Well, then. Let me take the tray in to him."

Pilot pricked up his ears when I walked through the door. He leaped to his feet and bounded across the room with an ecstatic yelp, almost knocking the tray from my hands.

"Down, Pilot," I said.

He sat reluctantly, his tail thumping hard on the floorboards.

"Mary?" Mr. Rochester asked. He turned his head toward me, straining to make his blind eyes see, but they would not. "Mary," he said again. "Is it you?"

"Mary's in the kitchen," I said.

"Who is this?" he demanded, trying again to see me with eyes that did not work.

"Mary knew me," I replied. "And Pilot recognizes me. Do you really not know who I am, sir?"

"I am ill," Mr. Rochester said. "I've lost my mind at last. I knew it would happen someday. Yet what a sweet fantasy this is. If this is illness, I never want to be sane."

"No fantasy," I told him. "No illness. I am here."

"Am I very ugly, Jane?" he asked.

"Hideous," I said. "But then, you always were."

"Elfish witch!" He reached a hand toward me and I took it in both of mine and kissed the palm.

"I have come back," I said. "And I will never leave again."

"But what will you be?" Mr. Rochester asked. "My nurse? My companion? You are young. Your life lies ahead, and I am crippled, Jane. I cannot see!"

"I'll be your right hand," I said, kissing his wrist from which the hand had once hung. "I'll be your eyes." I kissed both his eyelids. "I'll be your nurse." I kissed one cheek then the other. "And I'll be your companion, if that's what you wish. But I'd rather be your wife." My mouth hovered above his. "Mr. Rochester ... will you be mine?"

"Jane Eyre ... My plain Jane Eyre ... I will."

When Mary came in to take the tray away, we were kissing still.

Get lost in timeless classic retellings.

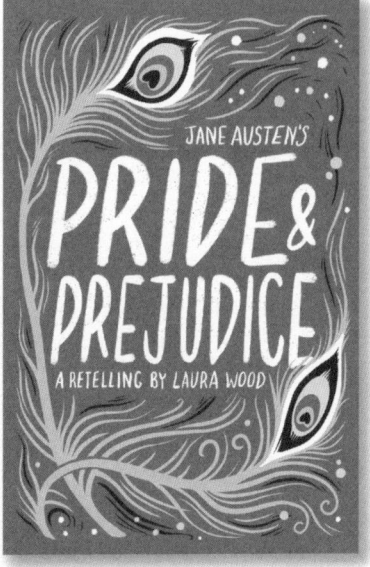

EVERYONE CAN BE A READER

32.

Reader, I married him.

And ten years have passed since then.

I am my husband's life and he is mine.

To be with him is to feel as free as if I were standing alone in the middle of the open moor on a bright spring day.

To be with him is to feel as joyfully merry as if I were in a warm room with the cheerful company of my dear friends and loving family.

We talk all day and half the night, and when we talk it is like thinking aloud. We are bone of each other's bone and flesh of each other's flesh. Our souls are one and the same.

And I am loved.

And I am wanted.

And I belong.